To Jaxon
♡ Evan

Japanese Children's Favorite Stories

JAPANESE CHILDREN'S FAVORITE STORIES

Florence Sakade

Illustrated by Yoshisuke Kurosaki

TUTTLE Publishing

Tokyo | Rutland, Vermont | Singapore

Published by Tuttle Publishing, an imprint of Periplus Editions (HK) Ltd.

www.tuttlepublishing.com

First printing of CD edition, 2005
Copyright © 1959 Charles E. Tuttle Co.
CD Recording © 2005 Charles E. Tuttle Co.
This anniversary edition copyright © 2013 Periplus Editions (HK) Ltd.
All rights reserved

LCC Card No. 58011620

ISBN 978-4-8053-1260-5

Printed in Malaysia

Distributed by:
Japan
Tuttle Publishing
Yaekari Building, 3F
5-4-12 Osaki, Shinagawa-ku, Tokyo 141-0032
Tel: (81)3 5437 0171; Fax: (81)3 5437 0755
sales@tuttle.co.jp; www.tuttle.co.jp

North America, Latin America & Europe
Tuttle Publishing
364 Innovation Drive
North Clarendon, VT 05759-9436 USA
Tel: 1(802) 773 8930; Fax: 1(802) 773 6993
info@tuttlepublishing.com; www.tuttlepublishing.com

Asia Pacific
Berkeley Books Pte Ltd
61 Tai Seng Avenue, #02-12
Singapore 534167
Tel: (65) 6280 1330; Fax: (65) 6280 6290
inquiries@periplus.com.sg; www.periplus.com

18 17 16 15   7 6 5 4 3 2   1503TWP

CONTENTS

PREFACE

Of the many Asian children's books Tuttle has been proud to publish over the years, *Japanese Children's Favorite Stories* is especially dear to our hearts and those of our readers.

And it's no wonder why. The stories in this classic treasury share a world in which good triumphs over evil, and where love, honesty, respect, hard work and determination carry with them great power. Statues come to life to repay kindness, and even a boy who is only one inch tall can become a great hero. The magic, after all, is around and within us all.

The same stories that have been loved by Japanese children for hundreds of years have also delighted western children through many printings and three editions of this book. Originally chosen from the pages of *Silver Bells*, the English language version of one of Japan's leading children's magazines of the 1950s, the 36 tales in these volumes range from fables with a clear moral to stories of action, adventure (and misadventure) and surprise. Each tale sparkles with fun and humor, and the whimsical illustrations bring to life a trove of enchanted people and places, wily animals and everyday folks with a flavor that is distinctly Japanese. Together, the stories and paintings have opened a window onto Japanese culture while sharing wisdom that has always transcended time and place.

Each of these stories is to be found in Japan—and often in other countries too—in many forms and versions. We have tried to select the most interesting version in each case and, in our translations, to remain true to the spirit of the Japanese originals. At the same time, we have tried to insert sufficient words of explanation into the text to allow Japanese customs and situations to be intelligible to western readers.

This new edition celebrates 60 years of bringing this very special part of Japanese culture to children in other parts of the world. Its steady success over the decades has shown time and again that stories that please children in one land are likely to please children everywhere, and that good stories say more about what we all have in common than about the things that separate us.

In the foreword to the original edition our founder Charles Tuttle wrote: "Parents and teachers all over the world have become increasingly aware of the need to raise their children to be citizens of the world, to become thinking adults who, while proud of their own traditions and heritage, are free of national prejudices, rivalries and suspicions that have caused such havoc in the past. To this end they have wanted material that would give their children a sympathetic understanding of the life and culture of other lands." It was to serve this need that *Japanese Children's Favorite Stories* was first published in 1953. Since then, bonds of friendship and family between East and West have grown stronger and deeper than ever before. But the need for literature that builds bridges between peoples and fosters in all of us— young and old—a sense of our interconnectedness is as great in the 21st century as it has been in times past. We hope that with these traditional tales new readers will experience joy in the universal power of story, and that parents and grandparents who have loved these tales as children will greet them as old friends and relive the magic as they share them with a new generation of readers.

PEACH BOY

Once upon a time there lived in Japan a kind old man and his wife. The old man was a woodcutter. He and his wife were very sad and lonely because they had no children.

One day the old man went into the mountains to cut firewood, and the old woman went to the river to wash clothes.

No sooner had the old woman begun her washing than she was very surprised to see a big peach floating down the river. It was the biggest peach she'd ever seen in all her life. She pulled the peach out of the river

and decided to take it home and share it with the old man for their supper that night.

Late in the afternoon the old man came home, and the old woman said to him, "Look what a wonderful peach I've found for our supper." The old man said it was truly a beautiful peach. He was very hungry and said, "Let's divide it and eat it right away."

So the old woman brought a big knife from the kitchen and got ready to cut the peach in half. But just then a human voice called out from inside the peach. "Wait! Don't cut me!" cried the voice. Suddenly the peach split open, and a beautiful baby boy jumped out of the peach.

The old man and woman were astounded. But the baby said, "Don't be afraid. The God of Heaven saw how lonely you were without any children, so he sent me to be your son."

The old man and woman were very happy, and they took the baby to be their son. Since he was born from a peach, they named him Momotaro, which means Peach Boy. They loved Momotaro very much and raised him to be a fine boy.

When Momotaro was fifteen years old, he said to his mother and father, "You have always been very kind to me. Now I am grown and I must do something to help our land. In a distant part of the sea is an island named Ogre Island. Many wicked ogres live there, and they often come here and do bad things like carrying people away and stealing our things. So I'm going to go to Ogre Island to fight them and bring back the treasures that they've stolen. Please let me do this!"

Momotaro's mother and father were surprised to hear this, but they were also very proud of Momotaro for wanting to help other people. So they helped Momotaro get ready for his journey to Ogre Island. The old man gave him a sword and some armor, and the old woman fixed him a good lunch of millet dumplings. Then Momotaro began his journey, promising his parents that he would be home soon.

Momotaro went walking toward the sea. It was a long way. As he went along, he met a brown dog. The dog growled at Momotaro and was about to bite him, but then Momotaro gave him one of his dumplings. He told the dog that he was going to fight the ogres on Ogre Island. So the brown dog said he would go along too to help Momotaro.

Momotaro and the brown dog kept on walking and soon they met a monkey. The dog and the monkey started to have a fight. But Momotaro told the monkey that they were going to fight the ogres on Ogre Island. Then the monkey asked if he could go with them. So Momotaro gave the monkey a dumpling and let him join them.

Momotaro, the brown dog and the monkey kept on walking and soon they met a pheasant. The dog, the monkey and the pheasant were about to start fighting when Momotaro told the pheasant they were going to fight the ogres on Ogre Island. The pheasant asked if he could go too. So Momotaro gave the pheasant a dumpling and told him to come along with them.

So, with Momotaro as their general, the brown dog, the monkey and the pheasant, who usually hated each other, became good and faithful friends.

They walked a long, long way, and finally reached the sea. There they built a boat and sailed across the sea to Ogre Island.

When they came within sight of the island, they could see that the ogres had a very strong fort there. And there were many, many ogres! Some of them were red, some were blue, and some were black.

First the pheasant flew over the walls of the fort and began to peck at the ogres' heads. The ogres tried to hit the pheasant with their clubs, but he was very quick and dodged their blows. While the ogres weren't looking, the monkey slipped into the fort and opened the gate. Then Momotaro and the brown dog rushed into the fort.

It was a terrible battle! The pheasant pecked at the heads of the wicked ogres, the monkey clawed at them with his nails, the brown dog bit them with his teeth, and Momotaro cut them with his sword.

At last the ogres were completely defeated. They bowed down before Momotaro and promised never to do wicked things again. Then they brought Momotaro all the treasure that they had stolen.

It was the most wonderful treasure you can imagine. There was gold and silver and many precious jewels. Momotaro and his three friends carried all of this back in their boat. Then they put the treasure in a cart and traveled throughout the land, returning to people all the treasure that the ogres had stolen.

Finally Momotaro returned to his own home. How happy his father and mother were to see him! They were very rich now with the remaining treasure that Momotaro had brought back, and they all lived together very, very happily.

THE MAGIC TEAKETTLE

There was once an old priest who was very fond of drinking tea. He always made the tea himself and was very fussy about the utensils he used. One day in an old secondhand shop he discovered a beautiful iron kettle used for boiling water for tea. It was a very old and rusty kettle, but the old priest could see its beauty beneath the rust. So he bought it and took it back to his temple. He polished the kettle until all the rust was gone, and then he called together his two young pupils, who lived with him in the temple.

"Just look at what a fine kettle I bought today," he said to them. "Now I'll boil some water with it and make us all some delicious tea."

So he put the kettle over a charcoal fire, and they all sat around waiting for the water to boil. The kettle started getting hotter and hotter, and then suddenly a very strange thing happened—the kettle grew the head of a tanuki, and a bushy tanuki tail, and four little tanuki feet!

"Ouch! It's hot!" cried the kettle. "I'm burning, I'm burning!" And with these words the kettle jumped off the fire and began running around the room on its tanuki feet.

The old priest was very surprised, but he didn't want to lose his kettle. "Quick! Quick!" he said to his two pupils, "Don't let it get away! Catch it!"

One pupil grabbed a broom and the other a pair of fire tongs. And away the two of them went, chasing after the kettle. When they finally caught it, the tanuki head and the bushy tanuki tail and the four little tanuki feet disappeared, and it became an ordinary kettle again.

"This is most strange," said the old priest. "This must be a bewitched teakettle! Now, we don't want anything like this around the temple. We must get rid of it."

Just then a junk dealer came by the temple. The old priest took the teakettle out to him and said, "Here's an old iron kettle I'd like to sell, Mr. Junkman. Just give me whatever you think it's worth."

The junk dealer weighed the kettle with his scale and then bought it from the old priest for a very low price. He went home whistling, pleased at having found such a bargain.

20

That night the junk dealer went to sleep and all the house was very quiet. Suddenly a voice called out, "Mr. Junkman! Oh, Mr. Junkman!"

The junk dealer opened his eyes. "Who's that calling me?" he said, lighting a lamp.

And there he saw the kettle, standing by his pillow, with a tanuki's head, and a bushy tanuki tail, and four little tanuki feet. The junk dealer said with surprise, "Aren't you the kettle I bought from the old priest today?"

"Yes, it's me," said the kettle. "But I'm not an ordinary kettle. I'm really a tanuki in disguise and my name is Bumbuku, which means 'good luck.' That old priest put me over a fire and burned me, so I ran away from him. But if you treat me kindly and feed me well and never put me over a fire, I'll stay with you and help you make your fortune."

"Why, this is very strange," said the junk dealer. "How can you help me make my fortune?"

"I can do all sorts of wonderful tricks," said the kettle, waving his bushy tanuki tail. "All you have to do is to put me in a show and sell tickets to the people who will come to see me perform."

The junk dealer thought this was a splendid idea. The very next day he built a little theater in his yard and put up a sign that said, "Bumbuku, The Magic Teakettle of Good Luck, and His Extraordinary Tricks!"

Every day more and more people came to see Bumbuku. The junk dealer would sell tickets and when the theater was full he would go inside and start beating a big drum. Bumbuku would come out and dance and do all sorts of acrobatics. The trick that pleased people most was when Bumbuku walked

across a tightrope carrying a paper parasol in one hand and a fan in the other. People found this most wonderful and would cheer and cheer for Bumbuku. And after every show the junk dealer would give Bumbuku delicious mochi cakes to eat.

The junk dealer sold so many tickets that he finally became a rich man. One day he said to Bumbuku, "You must be very tired of doing these tricks every day. I have all the money I need. Why don't I take you back to the temple, where you will be able to live quietly?"

"Well," said Bumbuku, "I am getting a little tired and wouldn't mind spending my time quietly in a temple. But that old priest might put me on the fire again, and he might never give me delicious mochi cakes."

"Just leave everything to me," said the junk dealer.

The next morning, the junk dealer took Bumbuku back to the temple. There he explained to the old priest everything that had happened and told him about the good fortune that Bumbuku had brought. When he had finished, the junk dealer asked, "So will you please let Bumbuku live here quietly, always feeding him mochi cakes and never putting him over the fire?"

"Indeed I will," said the old priest. "He shall have the place of honor in our treasure house. Bumbuku is truly a magic kettle of good luck, and I'd never have put him over the fire if I'd known!"

So the old priest called for his two pupils and together they placed Bumbuku on a wooden stand. Then they carried Bumbuku to the temple treasure house and placed some mochi cakes beside him.

It is said that Bumbuku is still there in the treasure house of the temple today, where he is very happy. He is given delicious mochi cakes to eat every day, and never, ever put over a fire. He is peaceful and happy.

MONKEY~DANCE AND SPARROW~DANCE

Once there was an old woodcutter who went so far into the mountains one day for firewood that he became lost. He walked for a long time, not knowing where he was going, until he suddenly heard music in the distance and smelled the wonderful aroma of food and drink.

Climbing to the top of a hill, the old woodcutter saw a great crowd of monkeys. They were eating and dancing and singing, and drinking a sake that they had made from rice. The sake smelled so good that the old woodcutter wanted some for himself.

The monkeys sang and danced beautifully, much to the old woodcutter's surprise. Then one of the monkeys filled a gourd with sake and told the other monkeys that it was time for him to go home. The other monkeys wished him farewell. The old woodcutter decided to follow the monkey to see if he could get some of the sake for himself.

Before long, the sake gourd grew too heavy for the monkey to carry. He stopped and poured some of the sake into a small jar. He put the jar on his head, balancing it carefully, then hid the gourd in the hollow of an old tree and went merrily on his way.

The old woodcutter had been watching all this from behind a tree. When the monkey was gone, he said to himself, "Surely the monkey won't mind if I just borrowed some of his sake." So he ran to the hollow tree and filled his own gourd with some of the sake. "This is wonderful," he thought. "If this sake tastes as good as it smells, it must be very fine indeed! I'll give this to my wife—*if* I can find my way home."

While the old woodcutter was lost in the mountains, his wife was having her own adventure. She was washing clothes under a tree when she noticed the sparrows above her having a party. They were drinking a sake that smelled so good the old woman just had to have some.

So, when the sparrows had finished dancing and singing, the old woman quickly tucked one of their sake gourds under her robe and hurried home. "I'll give this to my husband," she thought, "and if it tastes as good as it smells, it must be very fine indeed!"

No sooner had she arrived home than her husband also appeared, having finally found his way. "I have something for you!" they said at the same time. They told each other their amazing stories, then exchanged their sake gourds and drank deeply.

The sake tasted delicious. But no sooner had they drunk it than they both felt an uncontrollable desire to dance and sing. The old woman began to chatter and jump around like a monkey, while the old woodcutter held out his arms and chirped like a sparrow.

First the old woodcutter sang:

"One hundred sparrows dance in the spring,

Chirp-a chirp, chirp-a chirp, ching!"

Then the old woman sang:

"One hundred monkeys making a clatter,

Chatter-chat, chatter-chat, chatter!"

They made so much noise that their landlord came running to their house. There he saw the old woman dancing like a monkey, and the old woodcutter dancing like a sparrow.

"Here, here!" said the landlord. "This will never do! A woman's dance should be graceful and ladylike, like a sparrow's, and a man's dance should be bold and manly, like a monkey's! Not the other way round!"

When the old couple finally stopped dancing, they told the landlord their adventures. "Well, of course!" He said. "You've been drinking the wrong sake. Why don't you exchange gourds and see what happens."

After that the old woodcutter always drank the monkey sake, and danced in a very manly way. And the old woman always drank the sparrow sake, and danced in a very ladylike way. Everyone who saw them dance thought them very lovely and started imitating them. And that is why to this day men leap about nimbly and boldly when they dance, while women are much more graceful and birdlike when they dance.

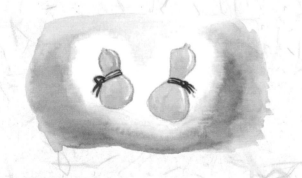

THE LONG-NOSED TENGUS

Long ago there were two long-nosed tengus who lived in the high mountains of northern Japan. One was a green tengu and the other a red tengu. They were both very proud of their noses, which they could extend for many, many leagues across the land, and they were always arguing as to who had the most beautiful nose.

One day the green tengu was resting on top of his mountain when he smelled something very good coming from somewhere down on the plains. "My, but something smells good," he said. "I wonder what it is!"

So he started extending his nose, making it grow longer and longer as it followed the smell. His nose grew so long that it crossed seven mountains, went down into the plains, and finally ended up at a great lord's mansion.

Inside the mansion, the lord's young daughter, Princess White Flower, was having a party. Many princesses had come to the party, and Princess White Flower was showing them her rare and beautiful kimono. They had opened the treasure house and taken out the wonderful clothes, all packed in incense. It was the incense that the green tengu had smelled.

Princess White Flower was looking for a place to hang her kimono so that everyone could see them better. When she caught sight of the green tengu's nose, she said, "Oh, look, someone's hung a green pole here. We'll hang the kimono on it!"

So the princess called her maids and they hung the beautiful kimono on the tengu's nose. The green tengu, sitting far away on his mountain, felt something tickling his nose, so he began pulling it back in.

When the princesses saw the beautiful kimono flying away through the air, they were very surprised. They tried to take back the kimono, but they were too late.

The green tengu was very pleased when he saw the beautiful kimono hanging from his nose. He gathered them up and took them home with him. Then he invited the red tengu, who lived on the next mountain, to come and see him.

"Just look what a wonderful nose I have," he said to the red tengu. "It's brought me all these wonderful kimono!"

The red tengu was jealous when he saw the kimono. He would have turned green with envy except that red tengus can't turn green.

"I'll show you whose nose is the best," the red tengu said. "Just you wait and I'll show you."

And so the red tengu sat on top of his mountain every day, rubbing his long red nose and sniffing the air. Many days passed and he still hadn't smelled anything good. He became very impatient and said, "Well, I won't wait any longer. I'll send my nose down to the plains anyway, and it's sure to find something good there."

So the red tengu started extending his nose, making it grow longer and longer, until it crossed seven mountains, went down into the plains, and finally ended up at the same lord's mansion.

At that moment the lord's young son, Prince Valorous, and his little friends were playing in the garden. When Prince Valorous caught sight of the red tengu's nose, he cried, "Look at this red pole that someone's put here. Let's use it as a swing!"

So the children tied some ropes to the red pole to make swings. Then how they played! They swung high up into the sky and climbed all over the red pole. One boy even cut his name into the pole with a knife.

How this hurt the red tengu, sitting back on his mountain! His nose was so heavy that he couldn't pull it back. But when his nose got cut, the red tengu shook the children off with all his might and pulled it back to his mountain as fast as he could.

The green tengu laughed and laughed at the sight. But the red tengu only sat stroking his nose and said, "This is what I get for being jealous. I'm never going to send my nose down into the plains again!"

THE RABBIT IN THE MOON

Once the Old-Man-of-the-Moon looked down into a big forest on the earth. He saw a rabbit, a monkey and a fox living there together in the forest as very good friends.

"Now, I wonder which of them is the kindest," said the Old Man to himself. "I think I'll go down and see."

So he changed himself into an old beggar and came down from the moon to the forest where the three friends were.

"Please help me," he said to them. "I'm very, very hungry."

34

"Oh! What a poor old beggar!" said the three friends, and they went hurrying off to find some food for him.

The monkey found and brought the beggar a lot of fruit. And the fox caught a big fish for him to eat. But the rabbit just couldn't find anything at all to bring.

"Oh my! Oh my! What shall I do?" the rabbit cried. But just then he had an idea.

"Please, Mr. Monkey," the rabbit said, "gather some firewood for me. And please, Mr. Fox, make a big fire with the firewood."

They did as their friend had asked, and when the fire was burning brightly, the rabbit said to the beggar, "I don't have anything to give you. So I'll put myself in this fire, and when I'm cooked you can eat me."

The rabbit was just about to jump into the fire when the beggar suddenly changed himself back into the Old-Man-of-the-Moon.

"You're very kind, Mr. Rabbit," he said, "but you should never do anything to harm yourself! Since you're the kindest of all, I'll take you home to live with me."

And then the Old-Man-of-the-Moon took the rabbit in his arms and carried him up to the moon. So when you look at the moon when it is shining brightly, you can still see the rabbit there where the Old Man took him so long ago.

THE TONGUE-CUT SPARROW

There was once a kind old farmer who had a very mean wife with a terrible temper. They didn't have any children, so the old farmer kept a tiny sparrow. He took loving care of the little bird, and when he came home from work every day he would pet and talk to it until suppertime, and then feed it with food from his own bowl. He treated the sparrow as if it were his own child.

But the old woman wouldn't ever show any kindness to anyone or anything. She particularly disliked the sparrow and was always scolding her husband for keeping such a nuisance around the house. Her temper was particularly bad on wash days, because she hated hard work.

One day while the old farmer was working in the field, the old woman got ready to do the washing. She had made some starch and set it in a wooden bowl to cool. While her back was turned, the sparrow hopped onto the edge of the bowl and pecked at the starch. Just then the old woman turned around and saw what the sparrow was doing. She became so angry that she grabbed a pair of scissors—and cut the sparrow's tongue right off! Then she threw the sparrow into the sky, crying, "Now get away from here, you nasty little bird!" And the poor sparrow went flying away into the woods.

A little while later the old farmer came home and found his sparrow gone. He looked and looked for it but couldn't find it. Finally the old woman

told him what she had done. The old farmer was very sad, and the next morning he started out into the forest to look for the sparrow. As he walked he kept calling, "Where are you, little sparrow? Where are you, little sparrow?"

Suddenly the sparrow came flying up to the old farmer. It was dressed in the kimono of a beautiful woman, and it spoke with a human voice. "Hello, my dear master," said the sparrow. "You must be very tired, so please come to my house and rest."

When the old farmer heard the sparrow speaking, he knew it must be a fairy sparrow. He followed the sparrow and came to a beautiful house in the forest. The sparrow had many daughters, and they prepared a feast for the old farmer, giving him many wonderful things to eat and drink. Four of the daughters performed a beautiful Sparrow-Dance. They danced so gracefully that the old farmer clapped and sang along.

Before the old farmer knew it, the sun had begun to set. When he saw that it was getting dark, he said he had to hurry home because his wife would be worried about him. The sparrow asked him to stay longer, and he was having such a good time that he didn't want to leave. But still he said, "No, I really must go."

"Well, then," said the sparrow, "for all your kindness to me, I would like to give you a gift to take home with you."

The sparrow brought out two baskets, one very big and heavy and the other small and light. "Please choose one," the sparrow said. The old farmer gratefully chose the small basket and started for home.

When he arrived home, the old farmer told his wife everything that had happened. When they opened the basket, it was full of wonderful things—gold and silver, diamonds and rubies, coral and coins. There was enough in the basket to make them rich for the rest of their lives.

The old farmer was very grateful for the treasure, but the old woman became angry. "You fool!" she said. "Why didn't you choose the big basket? Then we would've had much more. I'm going to the sparrow's house to get the other basket!"

The old farmer begged her not to be greedy, saying that they already had enough. But the old woman was determined. She put on her straw sandals and started off.

When she reached the sparrow's house, the old woman spoke very sweetly to the sparrow. The sparrow invited her into the house and gave her some tea. When the old woman stood up to leave, the sparrow again brought out a big basket and a small basket and told the woman to choose one as a gift. The old woman grabbed the big basket. It was so heavy she could hardly lift it up, but still she carried it and started home.

As she walked along, the basket became heavier and heavier. The old woman began wondering what treasures she would find in it. Finally she sat down by the path to rest, and her curiosity got the better of her. She just had to open the basket!

When she did, all sorts of terrible things jumped out at her! There was an ogre's head that made frightening noises, and a wasp that came flying at her with a long stinger, and snakes and toads and other slimy things! How frightened she was!

The old woman jumped up and ran as fast as she could all the way home. She told the old farmer what had happened, then said, "I promise never to be mean or greedy again!" And it seems she learned her lesson, because after that she became very kind and always helped the old farmer feed any birds that flew into their garden.

SILLY SABURO

Long ago there was a boy who lived on a farm in Japan. His name was Saburo, but he always did such silly things that people called him Silly Saburo. He could only remember one thing at a time, and then would do that one thing, no matter how silly it was. Saburo's father and mother were very worried for him, but they hoped he would get smarter as he grew older, and they were always very patient with him.

One day Saburo's father said to him, "Saburo, I need your help in the fields today. Please go to the potato patch and dig up the potatoes. After you've dug them up, spread them out carefully on the ground and leave them to dry in the sun."

"I understand, Father," said Saburo. And he put his hoe over his shoulder and went out to the potato patch.

Saburo was busy digging up the potatoes when all of a sudden his hoe hit something buried in the earth. He dug deeper and found a big pot that had been buried there. When he looked inside it he found many gold coins. It was a great treasure that someone had buried long ago.

"Father says I must dig things up and then leave them to dry in the sun," Saburo said to himself. So he very carefully spread the gold coins on the ground. When he got home, Saburo told his mother and father, "I found a pot of gold coins and spread them out in the sun to dry."

Saburo's father and mother were very surprised to hear this. They ran back to the potato patch, but someone had already taken the coins.

There was not a single coin left. "The next time you find something like this," Saburo's father said to him, "you must wrap it up very carefully and bring it home. Now don't forget!"

"I understand, Father," said Saburo.

The next day Saburo found a smelly cat in the field. He wrapped it up very carefully and brought it home with him, very proud of having remembered. But Saburo's father said to him, "Don't be so silly. The next time you find something like this, you must wash it in the river."

The next day Saburo dug up a huge tree stump. He thought very hard and remembered what his father had said about the smelly cat. So he took the stump and threw it with a great splash into the river.

Just then a neighbor was passing by and said, "You mustn't throw away valuable things like that! That stump would have made good firewood. You should have broken it up into pieces and taken it home."

"I understand," said Saburo, and started on his way home. Along the way he saw a teapot and teacup that somebody had left beside the road.

"Oh, here's something valuable!" said Saburo. So he took his hoe and broke the teapot and teacup into small pieces. Then he gathered up all the pieces and took them home with him.

"Hello, Mother," he said. "Look what I found and brought home." Then he showed his mother the broken pieces of the teapot and teacup.

"Oh, my!" said Saburo's mother. "That's the brand-new teapot and teacup I gave your father to take with his lunch today. And now you've completely ruined them!"

The next day Saburo's father and mother said to him, "Everything you do, you do wrongly. We'll go out into the fields and work today. Stay home and take care of the house." So they left Saburo alone at home.

"I really don't understand why people call me Silly Saburo," Saburo said to himself. "I do exactly what people tell me to do!"

THE TOOTHPICK WARRIORS

Once upon a time there was a beautiful princess who had a very bad habit. Every night before she slept she would lie in bed and pick her teeth with a toothpick. That wasn't so bad, but after she was done, instead of throwing away the used toothpicks as she should have, she would stick them between the cracks of the straw mats where she slept. Now, this was not a very clean habit, and since the princess did this every night, the cracks of her straw mats were soon filled with dozens and dozens of used toothpicks.

One night the princess was suddenly awakened by the sound of fighting. She heard the voices of warriors and the sound of swords. Frightened, she sat up and lit the lamp beside her bed. She could hardly believe what she saw.

There, right beside her quilt, were many tiny warriors! Some were fighting, some were singing and some were dancing, but all of them were making a great deal of noise.

The princess thought that she was dreaming, so she pinched herself hard. But, no, she was wide awake, and the tiny warriors were still there! Though they didn't bother the princess, they made so much noise all night that she couldn't sleep at all, and when she finally did doze off, she suddenly woke up again because it was so quiet. It was morning and the tiny warriors were gone.

The princess was very afraid, but she was ashamed to tell the lord, her father, because he wouldn't have believed her. Yet when she went to bed the following night, the tiny warriors appeared again, and again the night after that.

In fact, the tiny warriors made so much noise every night that the princess couldn't get any sleep, and each day she became a little paler. Soon she became quite ill from not sleeping.

The princess' father kept asking her what the matter was, and finally she told him. At first he didn't believe her story, but he finally decided to see for himself. He told her to sleep in his room that night and he would stand watch in hers.

And so he did. But though he remained awake all night and watched and waited, the tiny warriors did not come.

While waiting, however, the princess' father noticed a toothpick on the straw mat. He picked it up and looked carefully at it, then called the princess to him the next morning.

He showed her one of the toothpicks. It was all cut up but the marks were so tiny that the princess could barely see them. She asked her father what the marks meant. Her father explained that the tiny warriors had come to her room because of all the used toothpicks! The warriors had no swords of their own and toothpicks made the best swords, and this was why they had come to the princess' room every night!

The warriors hadn't come last night, he said, because he had been there, and they were afraid. Then the princess' father looked at her sternly and asked why there were so many used toothpicks in her room.

The princess was very ashamed of her bad habit, and she admitted to her father that it was she who had stuck the toothpicks between the cracks in the straw mats, because she had been too lazy to throw them away. She also said she was very, very sorry and promised that she would never, ever be so lazy again.

Then she picked up all the toothpicks in her room, even those at the very bottom of the cracks, and threw them all away. That night the warriors did not come because there were no tiny swords for them, and they never came again.

Soon the princess felt better again because the warriors no longer kept her awake. She became very neat about everything, and pleased her father greatly by even sweeping the garden every day. She never forgot the tiny warriors, and if she ever used a toothpick again, you may be sure that she was very careful to throw it away properly.

THE STICKY-STICKY PINE

Once there was a young woodcutter who lived in Japan. He was very poor but kind-hearted. Whenever he went to gather firewood, he would never tear off the living branches of a tree, but would instead gather the dead branches that had fallen on the ground. This was because the kind woodcutter knew what would happen if you tore a branch off a tree. The sap, which is like the blood of a tree, would drip and drip, as though the poor tree was bleeding. Since the woodcutter didn't want to hurt any trees, he never tore off any of their branches.

One day the woodcutter was walking beneath a tall pine tree looking for firewood when he heard a voice saying:

"Sticky, sticky is my sap,

For my tender twigs are snapped."

The woodcutter looked around, and sure enough, someone had broken three branches off the pine tree and its sap was running out.

Skillfully, the woodcutter mended the broken branches, saying:

"Now these tender twigs I'll wrap,

And in that way I'll stop the sap."

He tore pieces from his own clothes to make bandages. No sooner had he finished than many tiny gold and silver things fell from the tree. They were coins! The surprised woodcutter could not believe his eyes. He looked up at the pine tree and thanked it. Then he gathered up all the coins and took them home.

The kind woodcutter had so many gold and silver coins that he knew he was now a very rich man. Pine trees are a symbol of prosperity in Japan, and, sure enough, the grateful pine tree had repaid him for his kind act.

Just then a face appeared at the window of the woodcutter's house. It belonged to another woodcutter. But this woodcutter was neither nice nor kind. In fact, it was he who had torn off the three branches from the pine tree. When he saw the coins, he asked, "Where did you get all those coins? Look how nice and bright they are."

The kind woodcutter held up the coins for the other to see. They were oblong in shape, the way coins used to be in Japan, and he had five basketfuls. He told the mean woodcutter how he had got the coins.

"From that big pine tree?" asked the mean woodcutter.

"Yes, that was the one."

"Hmm," said the mean woodcutter and away he ran as fast as he could. He wanted some of the coins for himself.

54

The mean woodcutter came to the old pine tree, and the tree said:

"Sticky, sticky, is my blood.

Touch me, you'll receive a flood."

"Oh, that's just what I want," said the mean woodcutter. "A flood of gold and silver!" He reached up and broke off another branch. The pine tree suddenly showered him. But it showered him with sticky, sticky sap—not gold and silver at all!

The mean woodcutter was covered with the sap. It got in his hair and on his arms and legs. It was so sticky, he couldn't move at all. Though he called for help, no one could hear him. He had to remain there for three days—one day for each branch that he had broken—until the sap became soft enough for him to drag himself home.

And, after that, he never broke another branch off a living tree.

THE SPIDER WEAVER

Long ago there was a young farmer named Yosaku. One day he was working in the fields and saw a snake about to eat a spider. Yosaku felt sorry for the spider, so he ran at the snake with his hoe and drove it away.

The spider disappeared into the grass, but first it seemed to pause a moment and bow in thanks toward Yosaku.

One morning not long after that, Yosaku was in his house when he heard a tiny voice outside calling, "Yosaku, Yosaku!" He opened the door and saw a beautiful girl standing there.

"I heard that you are looking for someone to weave cloth for you," said the girl. "Won't you please let me live here and weave for you?"

Yosaku was very pleased because he did need someone to help him. He showed the girl the weaving room and she started to work at the loom with cotton. At the end of the day Yosaku went to see what she had done, and was very surprised to find that she had woven eight long pieces of cloth, enough to make eight kimono. He had never known anyone could weave so much in a single day.

"However did you weave so much cloth?" he asked the girl.

But instead of answering him, she said, "You mustn't ask me that. And you must never come into the weaving room while I am at work."

But Yosaku was very curious. So one day he slipped quietly to the weaving room and peeped in the window. What he saw really surprised him! It was not the girl who was seated at the loom, but a large spider, weaving very fast with its eight legs, and for thread it was using its own spiderweb, which came out of its mouth.

Yosaku looked again and saw that it was the same spider that he had saved from the snake. Then he understood. The spider had been so thankful that it had wanted to do something to help him. So it had turned itself into a beautiful girl to help him weave cloth. By eating the cotton that was in the weaving room, it could spin it into thread and weave it into cloth very, very quickly.

Yosaku was very grateful for the spider's help. He saw that the cotton was almost used up, so the next morning he set out for the nearest village,

on the other side of the mountains, to buy some more. He bought a big bundle of cotton and started home, carrying it on his back.

Along the way a terrible thing happened. As Yosaku sat down to rest, the same snake that he'd driven away from the spider came and slipped inside the bundle of cotton. But Yosaku didn't know about this. So he carried the cotton home and gave it to the girl.

She was very glad to get the cotton, because she had now used up all the cotton that was left. So she took it and went to the weaving room.

As soon as the girl was inside the weaving room she turned back into a spider and began eating the cotton so that she could spin it into thread. The spider ate and ate and ate, and then suddenly, when it had eaten down to the bottom of the bundle—the snake jumped right out of the cotton and straight at her!

The snake opened its mouth wide to swallow the spider. The spider was very frightened and jumped out the window, but the snake went wriggling after it. But the spider had eaten so much cotton that it couldn't run fast, and the snake soon caught up with it. Again the snake opened its mouth wide to gulp the spider down. But just then a wonderful thing happened.

Old Man Sun, up in the sky, had been watching what was happening. He knew how kind the spider had been to Yosaku and he felt very sorry for the poor little spider. So he reached down with a sunbeam and caught hold of the end of the web that was sticking out of the spider's mouth, and he gently lifted the spider high up into the sky, where the snake couldn't reach her.

60

The spider was very grateful to Old Man Sun for saving her from the snake. And so she used all the cotton inside her body to weave many beautiful, fleecy clouds high up in the sky.

This is the reason, they say, why clouds are soft and white like cotton, and also why a spider and a cloud are both called by the same name in Japan—kumo.

LITTLE ONE~INCH

There was once a kindly couple who had no children. One day they went to a shrine and prayed for a baby, saying, "Oh, please give us a child. We want a child very badly."

On their way home from the shrine, they heard a tiny crying sound coming from a patch of grass. They looked in the grass, and there they found a tiny little baby boy, wrapped in a bright red blanket. "This child has come in answer to our prayers," they said. So they took the little baby home with them and raised him as their son.

Now this baby was so tiny that he wasn't as large as your thumb, and even as he grew older he stayed the same size. He was just about an inch tall, so the couple named him Little One-Inch.

One day, when he had grown older, Little One-Inch said to his mother and father, "Thank you very much for raising me so well. But now I must go out into the world and make my fortune."

The couple tried to keep him from leaving, saying he was too tiny to go out into the world. But Little One-Inch insisted, so finally they said, "All right, we'll help you get ready." And they gave him a needle to use for a sword, a rice bowl to use for a boat, and a chopstick to use for an oar.

Little One-Inch got in his boat and waved goodbye to his parents, promising to return home when he had made his fortune. Then he went floating down the river in his rice bowl boat, paddling with his chopstick.

Little One-Inch had floated along for many, many leagues when a frog accidentally knocked into his boat and turned it over. Little One-Inch was a very good swimmer and he swam to the riverbank, where he found himself standing before a great lord's house.

Little One-Inch looked at the house and saw that it must belong to a very wealthy lord. He walked boldly up to the front door and called out. A servant came to the door, but he couldn't see anyone.

"Here I am, down here!" cried Little One-Inch. "Look down here!"

The servant looked down at the ground. At first all he could see was a pair of wooden sandals that his lord used when he went out walking. Then the servant looked closer and saw the tiny figure of Little One-Inch standing beside the sandals. He was so surprised that he hurried off to tell his lord.

The lord came to the front door himself and looked down at Little One-Inch standing there proudly, his needle-sword at his hip. "Why, hello there, little warrior," he said. "What do you want here?"

"I've come out into the world to seek my fortune," said Little One-Inch. "And if you'll have me, let me become one of your guards. I may be small, but I can fight very well with this fine sword."

The lord was very amused to hear the tiny boy speak such bold words. "All right," he said, "you can come and be a playmate for my daughter, the princess."

So Little One-Inch became the companion of the princess. They soon became good friends, reading and playing together every day. The princess even made a bed for Little One-Inch in her jewel box.

One day Little One-Inch and the princess went to visit a temple near the lord's house. Suddenly, a terrible green devil appeared, carrying a magic hammer. When the devil saw the princess he ran toward her to carry her off.

Little One-Inch quickly drew his needle-sword and began sticking the green devil's toes with it. But the devil's skin was so thick that the tiny sword couldn't go through it. As the devil got closer to the princess, Little One-Inch climbed up the devil's body and out onto his arm. Then he waved his sword at the devil's nose. This made the devil so angry that he opened his mouth wide to let out a roar.

At that moment Little One-Inch gave a big leap and jumped right onto the green devil's face and began poking his nose with the sword. Now the devil's nose was very tender and the needle hurt very much. He was so surprised that he jumped up, yelled and went running away. He even dropped his magic hammer.

The princess said, "Thank you, Little One-Inch," and picked up the magic hammer. "Now we can use this to make a wish!" She shook the hammer in the air and said, "Please let Little One-Inch grow taller!"

Sure enough, each time she shook the hammer, Little One-Inch grew one inch taller. The princess kept shaking it until he was just as tall as she was. They were both very happy, and the lord was very grateful when he heard what Little One-Inch had done.

When they were a few years older, Little One-Inch and the princess were married, and they lived very happily ever after.

THE TANUKI AND THE MAGIC FAN

In Japan, goblins are called tengus and they all have very long noses. Now I once upon a time three little tengu children were playing in the forest. They had a magic fan with them, and when they fanned their noses with one side of the fan, their noses would grow longer and longer, and when they fanned their noses with the other side, their noses would shrink back to their original sizes.

The three tengu children were having a wonderful time fanning their noses. But just then a tanuki came by and saw what they were doing. "My!

How I'd like to have a fan like that!" he said to himself. And then he thought of a good trick. Tanukis are always playing tricks and can change themselves into any shape they want. So the tanuki changed himself into a little girl. He took four bean-jam buns with him and went to the tengu children.

"Hello, children," said the tanuki. "I've brought you some wonderful bean-jam buns. Please let me play with you!"

The tengu children were delighted because they loved to eat bean-jam buns. But there were four delicious buns to be divided among the three of them, and they immediately started arguing over who would get the very last bun.

Finally the tanuki said, "I know how to decide who gets the last bun. Close your eyes, and the one who can keep his eyes closed and hold his breath the longest will win the last bun."

The tengu children all agreed. The tanuki counted, "One! Two! Three!" and they closed their eyes hard. As soon as they did, the tanuki grabbed the

magic fan and went running away with it as fast as he could, leaving the tengu children in the forest with their eyes closed and still holding their breath.

"Ha, ha, ha!" laughed the tanuki. "I certainly made fools out of those tengu children!" he said, and went walking along his way.

Soon the tanuki came to a temple. There he saw a beautiful girl dressed in very expensive clothes. He felt sure she was the daughter of a wealthy man, and in fact her father was a great lord and the richest man in all of Japan. So the tanuki crept up quietly behind her on tiptoe. Quick as a flash he fanned her nose with the magic fan. Instantly her nose grew a yard long!

What a terrible to-do there was! Here was the beautiful little rich girl with the nose a yard long! Her father called all the doctors in the land, but none of them could do anything to make her nose shorter. He spent a lot

70

of money on medicines, but nothing did any good. Finally in desperation he said, "I'll give my daughter as a wife and half my fortune to anyone who can make her nose grow short again!"

When the tanuki heard this, he said, "That's what I've been waiting for." He quickly went to the great lord and announced that he had come to fix her nose. So the great lord took the tanuki to his daughter's room. The tanuki took out the magic fan and fanned her nose with the other side of it. In the twinkling of an eye her nose was short again!

The great lord was very happy and started making preparations for the wedding. The tanuki was very happy too because not only was he going to get a beautiful wife, he was also going to get a large fortune.

On the day of the wedding, the tanuki was so happy that he ate and drank too much and became very hot and sleepy. Without thinking, he lay back on some pillows, closed his eyes and began fanning himself with the magic fan. Instantly his nose began to grow longer. But as he was half asleep, he didn't know this was happening. So he kept fanning and fanning himself and his nose kept on growing and growing. It went right through the ceiling and high into the sky until it pierced the clouds.

Now, above the clouds some
heavenly workers were building a bridge
across the Milky Way. "Look at that!" they
cried, pointing to the tanuki's nose. "That
pole's just the right size for our bridge.
Come on, let's pull it up!"

And they began pulling on the tanuki's
nose. How this surprised the tanuki! He
started out of his sleep, crying, "Ouch! Help,
help!" And he began to fan his nose
with the other side of the fan as fast
as he possibly could.

But it was much too late. The
heavenly workers kept on pulling, crying,
"Heave, ho!" until they had pulled the tanuki
into the sky, and no one ever saw him
again.

MR. LUCKY STRAW

Once upon a time, long ago, there was a good-hearted young man named Shobei who lived in a village in Japan.

One day on his way home from working in the fields, Shobei fell down the steps that led to his village and tumbled over and over on the ground. When he finally stopped tumbling, Shobei discovered that he had caught a piece of straw in his hand.

"Well, well," he said, "a piece of straw is a worthless thing, but it seems I was meant to pick this one up, so I won't throw it away."

As Shobei went walking along, holding the straw in his hand, a dragonfly came flying in circles around his head. "What a pest!" he said. "I'll show this dragonfly not to bother me!" And he caught the dragonfly and tied the straw around its tail.

Shobei went on walking, holding on to the dragonfly, and presently met a woman walking with her son. When the little boy saw the dragonfly, he wanted it very badly. "Mother, I want that dragonfly," he said. "Please, please, please!"

"Here you are, little boy, you can have my dragonfly!" said Shobei, handing the boy the straw. To thank Shobei, the little boy's mother gave him three oranges. Shobei thanked her and went on his way.

Before long, Shobei met a peddler resting by the road. The peddler was so thirsty that he was about to faint. There were no streams nearby and Shobei felt very sorry for the peddler, so he gave him the three oranges so that he could drink the juice.

The peddler was very grateful, and in exchange he gave Shobei three pieces of cloth that he was carrying to market. Shobei thanked him and went on his way.

As Shobei was walking along, he came across a fine carriage with many attendants. The carriage belonged to a princess who was on her way to town. The princess just happened to look out of the carriage and saw the beautiful pieces of cloth that Shobei was carrying. She said, "Oh, what pretty pieces of cloth you have there. Please let me have them." Shobei gave the princess the three pieces of cloth, and to thank him, she gave him a large bag of coins.

Shobei took the coins and bought many fields with them. Then he divided the fields among the people of his village. Thus everyone had his or her own piece of land, and they all worked hard on them. The village became very prosperous and many new houses were built. Everyone was amazed when they remembered that all this wealth came from the piece of straw that Shobei had picked up.

Shobei became the most important man in the village and everyone respected him greatly. And for as long as he lived, they all addressed him as "Mr. Lucky Straw."

WHY THE JELLYFISH
HAS NO BONES

Long ago all the sea creatures lived happily in the palace of the Dragon King, deep at the bottom of the sea—well, almost all of them. The octopus, who was the palace doctor, disliked the jellyfish immensely. In those days, the jellyfish still had bones like all the other creatures.

One day the daughter of the Dragon King became sick. The octopus came to see her and said she would die unless she took a medicine made from the liver of a monkey. "The jellyfish is a good swimmer," said the octopus to the king, "so why not send him to find a monkey's liver?"

And so the king called the jellyfish and sent him on the important errand. But finding a monkey's liver wasn't easy. Even finding a monkey was difficult. The jellyfish swam and swam for days and finally, near a little island, he found a monkey who had fallen in the sea.

"Help, help!" called out the monkey, who couldn't swim.

"I'll help you," said the jellyfish, "But in return you must promise to give me your liver so that we can make a medicine for the Dragon King's daughter." The monkey promised, so the jellyfish carried him on his back and went swimming away toward the palace.

The monkey had been willing to promise anything while he was drowning, but now that he was safe he began to think about his promise. The more he thought, the less he liked the idea of giving up his liver, even for the Dragon King's daughter. No, he decided, he didn't like it one little bit. Being a very clever monkey, he said, "Wait, wait! I just remembered that I left my liver hanging on a tree branch back on the island. Take me back there and I'll get it for you."

So the jellyfish returned to the island. The monkey climbed up a tall tree and then called out to the jellyfish, "Thank you very much for saving me! I can't find my liver anywhere, but I'll just stay here, thank you!"

The jellyfish realized that he had been tricked, but there was nothing he could do about it. He swam slowly back to the palace at the bottom of the sea and told the Dragon King what had happened. The king was very angry.

"Let me and the other fish beat this no-good fellow for you," said the wicked octopus to the king.

"All right, beat him hard," said the king.

So they beat the jellyfish until all his bones were broken. He cried and cried, and the octopus laughed and laughed.

Just then the princess came running in. "Look!" she cried, "I'm not sick at all. I just had a little stomach-ache."

The Dragon King realized that the octopus had lied to them so that he could get even with his enemy, the jellyfish. The king became so furious that he sent the octopus away from the palace forever and made the jellyfish his favorite. So this is why the octopus now lives alone, scorned and feared by all who live in the sea. And this is why, even though he still has no bones and can no longer swim quickly, the jellyfish is never bothered by the other creatures of the sea.

THE OLD MAN WHO
MADE TREES BLOSSOM

Once upon a time there was a very kind old man and his wife who lived
in a small village in Japan. Next door to them lived a very mean old
man and his wife. The kind old couple had a little white dog named Shiro.
They loved Shiro very much and always gave him good things to eat. But
the mean old man hated dogs, and every time he saw Shiro he would throw
stones at him.

One day Shiro was barking loudly in the yard. The kind old man went
out to see what was the matter. Shiro kept barking and barking and began

digging in the ground. "Oh, do you want me to help you dig?" asked the old man. He brought a spade and began digging. Suddenly his spade hit something hard. He dug deeper and found a small pot of gold buried in the earth! The kind old man took it into his house and thanked Shiro for leading him to the gold.

Now the mean old man and his wife had been spying on their neighbor and had seen all this. They wanted some gold for themselves. So the next day the mean old man asked if he could borrow Shiro for a while. "Why, of course you may borrow Shiro, if he can be of any help to you," said the kind old man.

The mean old man took Shiro out to his field. "Now find me some gold too," he ordered the dog, "or I'll beat you." So Shiro began digging at a spot on the ground. The mean old man tied Shiro to a tree and began digging for himself. But all he found was some terrible-smelling garbage! This made him so angry that he hit Shiro on the head with his spade, and killed him.

The kind old man and his wife were very sad about Shiro. They buried him in their field and planted a pine tree over his grave. And every day they went to Shiro's grave and watered the pine tree lovingly.

The tree began to grow very quickly, and in only a short time it became very big. The kind old woman said, "Remember how Shiro used to love to eat mochi cakes? Let's cut down the tree and make a mortar from its trunk. Then with the mortar we'll make some mochi cakes in memory of Shiro." So the kind old man cut down the tree and made a mortar. He filled it full of steamed rice and began pounding it to make mochi cakes. But no sooner had he begun pounding than all the rice turned into gold! Now the kind old man and his wife were richer than ever.

The mean old man and his wife had been peeping through the window and had seen the rice turn to gold. They wanted some gold for themselves. So the next day the mean old man asked if he could borrow the mortar. "Why, of course you may borrow it," said the kind old man.

The mean old man took the mortar home and filled it full of steamed rice. "Now watch," he said to his wife. "When I begin pounding this rice, it will turn into gold." But when he began pounding, the rice turned instead into terrible-smelling garbage! This made him so angry that he chopped the mortar up and burned the pieces in his fireplace.

When the kind old man went to get his mortar back, it was burned to ashes. He was very sad because the mortar had reminded him of Shiro. So he asked for some of the ashes and took them home with him.

It was the middle of winter and all the trees were bare. The kind old man decided to scatter some of the ashes in his garden. When he did this, all the cherry trees in the garden suddenly began to bloom. Everybody came to see this wonderful sight, and even the prince who lived in a nearby castle heard about it.

Now the prince had a cherry tree that he loved very much. Each year he could hardly wait for spring to come so that he could see its beautiful cherry blossoms. But when spring had come that year he discovered that the tree was dead and he was very sad. Now he sent for the kind old man and asked him to bring his tree back to life.

The old man took some of the ashes and climbed up the tree. Then he threw the ashes up into the dead branches, and before they knew it, the

whole tree was covered with the most beautiful cherry blossoms that they had ever seen.

The prince was very pleased. He gave the kind old couple a great box of gold and many presents. Best of all, he gave the old man a new title, "Sir Old-Man-Who-Makes-Trees-Blossom."

Sir Old-Man-Who-Makes-Trees-Blossom and his wife were now very rich, and they lived very happily for many more years.

THE CRAB AND THE MONKEY

Once a crab and a monkey went for a walk together. Along the way the monkey found a persimmon seed, and the crab found a rice ball. The monkey wanted the crab's rice ball, and being a very clever talker, he finally persuaded the crab to trade the rice ball for the persimmon seed. The monkey quickly ate the rice ball.

The crab couldn't eat the persimmon seed, but he took it home and planted it in his garden, where it began to grow. Because the crab watered it carefully every day, it grew and grew.

The tiny seed finally became a big tree, and one autumn day the crab saw that it was full of beautiful persimmons. The crab wanted very much to eat the persimmons, but no matter how hard he tried, he couldn't climb the tree. So he asked his friend the monkey to pick the persimmons for him.

Now, the monkey loved persimmons even more than rice balls, and once he was up the tree he began eating all the ripe persimmons, and the only ones he threw down to the crab were hard and unripe. One of them hit the crab on the head and hurt him badly.

The crab was angry and asked three of his friends, a mortar and a hornet and a chestnut, to help him punish the monkey. So the three friends hid themselves around the crab's house one day, and the crab invited the monkey to come to tea.

When the monkey arrived he was given a seat by the fireplace. The chestnut was hiding in the ashes roasting himself, and suddenly he burst out of the fireplace and burned the monkey on his neck. The monkey screamed with pain and jumped up.

In an instant the hornet flew down and stung the monkey with his tail. The monkey tried to run away, but the mortar was hiding above the door and fell down with a thud on the monkey, hurting his back.

The monkey saw there was no escape. He bowed down to the crab and his three friends and said, "I did a bad thing when I ate the Crab's delicious persimmons and threw the unripe ones to him. I promise never to do such a bad thing again. Please forgive me!"

The crab accepted the monkey's apology, and they became friends again. The monkey learned his lesson and never again cheated anyone.

THE OGRE AND THE ROOSTER

There once was a mountain so high and steep that it seemed to touch the sky. On top of this mountain lived a terrible ogre. He had red skin and a single horn growing out of his head, and he was always doing wicked things to the village people at the foot of the mountain.

One morning the farmers of the village who worked at the foot of the mountain went to their fields and saw their vegetables ruined. Someone had pulled them all up and had trampled on them until there was not a single good one left.

They wondered who could have done such a thing, then saw the ogre's footprints all over the ground.

This made the farmers angry. They were tired of the ogre's tricks, and when they looked at all the ruined vegetables they became angrier. They pointed up at the mountain and cried, "Oh, you wicked ogre! Why don't you quit doing these wicked things?"

The ogre looked down at them from the top of the mountain and answered in a terrible voice, "You must give me a human every day for my supper. Then I'll stop bothering you!"

The farmers had never heard of such a request. They shook their tools at the ogre and shouted back, "Who do you think you are, wanting to eat a human every day?"

"I'm the ogre-est ogre in the land," the ogre roared back. "That's who I am! There's absolutely nothing I can't do! Ha, ha, ha!" The ogre's voice

echoed loudly through the mountains and made all the trees bend and sway.

"All right then," yelled back the farmers. "Let's see how great you really are! If you can build a stone stairway with a hundred steps in one night, from our fields all the way to the top of the mountain, then we'll do whatever you want."

"Why, I can do that!" the ogre replied. "And if I haven't finished the stairway before the first rooster crows tomorrow morning, then I promise to go away and to never bother you again."

As soon as it grew dark, the ogre crept into the village and put a straw hood over the head of every single rooster so it wouldn't see the sun rising. Then the ogre thought to himself, "Now I'll build that stairway!" And he set to work, building the stairway up the mountain.

The ogre worked so hard and so quickly that he already had ninety-nine steps in place when the sun began to rise in the east. But he only smiled to himself, thinking that the roosters wouldn't be able to crow and that he still had plenty of time to put the last step in place.

But a kind fairy also lived on the mountain. The fairy had been watching the ogre and had seen the mean trick he was playing. So while the ogre was going down the stairway for the last stone, the fairy flew down and took the straw hood off the head of one of the roosters.

The rooster saw the sun rising and crowed loudly, "ko-ke-kok-ko!" This woke up all the other roosters, and they all began to crow.

The ogre was surprised to hear this. "I've lost!" he cried. "And there was just one more step to go." But even ogres must keep their promises, so he stroked his horn very sadly and went far away into the mountains.

No one ever saw the ogre again and the farmers lived very happily at the foot of the mountain. They finished the stairway up the mountain and often climbed it on summer evenings to enjoy the wonderful view.

THE RABBIT WHO
CROSSED THE SEA

Once there was a white rabbit who wanted to cross the sea. Across the waves he could see a beautiful island and he wanted very badly to go there. But the rabbit couldn't swim and there were no boats around. Then he had an idea.

He called to a shark in the sea and said, "Oh, Mr. Shark, which one of us has the most friends, you or I?"

"I'm sure I have the most friends," said the shark.

"Well, let's count them to make sure," said the rabbit. "Why don't you

have all your friends line up in the sea between here and that island? Then I can count them."

So all the sharks lined up in the sea, and the rabbit went hopping from the back of one shark to the next, counting, "One, two, three, four, five . . . ." Finally he reached the island.

Then he turned to the sharks and said, "Ha, ha, you dumb sharks! I certainly fooled you. I got you to make a bridge for me, without you knowing about it."

The sharks became very angry. One of them reached up with his sharp teeth and bit off a piece of the rabbit's fur.

"Oh, that hurts!" cried the rabbit and he began weeping.

Just then the king of the island came by. He asked the rabbit what was the matter, and when he had heard the rabbit's story, he said, "You mustn't ever fool others and tell lies again. If you promise to be good, I'll tell you how you can get your fur back."

"Oh, I promise, I promise," said the rabbit.

So the king gathered some bulrushes and made a nest with them. "Now you sleep here in this nest of bulrushes all night," said the king, "and your fur will grow back."

The rabbit did as he was told. The next morning he went to the king and said, "Thank you very, very much. My fur grew back and I'm well again. Thank you, thank you, thank you."

Then the rabbit went hopping off along the seashore, dancing and singing. He never tried to fool anyone again.

THE GRATEFUL STATUES

Once upon a time there lived a kind old couple in a village in Japan. They were very poor and spent every day weaving hats out of straw. Whenever they finished a number of hats, the old man would take them to the nearest town to sell.

One day the old man said to the old woman, "It will be New Year's Day in two days. How I wish we had some mochi cakes to eat then! Even one or two little cakes would be enough. Without mochi cakes we won't be able to celebrate the new year."

"Well, then," said the old woman, "after you've sold these hats we're making, buy some mochi cakes for New Year's Day."

So early the next morning the old man took the five new hats that they had made and went to town to sell them. But when he got to town he was unable to sell a single hat. And to make things worse, it began to snow very heavily.

The old man felt very sad as he trudged wearily home with his hats. He was walking down a lonesome mountain trail when he suddenly came upon a row of six stone statues of Jizo, the protector of children, all covered in thick snow.

"My, my! Now isn't this a pity," said the old man. "These are only stone statues of Jizo, but even so, just think how cold they must be, standing here in the snow."

"I know what I'll do!" said the old man to himself. He unfastened the five new hats from his back and began tying them, one by one, onto the heads of the statues.

When he came to the last statue he suddenly realized that all the new hats had been used. "Oh, my!" he said, "I don't have enough hats." But then he remembered his own scarf. So he took it off his head and tied it on the head of the last statue. Then he went on his way home.

When he got home the old woman was waiting for him by the fire. She took one look at him and cried, "You must be frozen half to death! Quick, come sit by the fire. What did you do with your scarf?"

The old man shook the snow out of his hair and came to the fire. He told the old woman how he had given all the new hats as well as his own scarf to the six Jizo statues. He also said he was sorry that he hadn't been able to bring home any mochi cakes.

"That was a very kind thing you did for the statues," said the old woman. She was very proud of the old man and said, "It's better to do a kind thing like that than to have all the mochi cakes in the world. We'll get along without any mochi cakes for New Year's Day."

Since it was already late at night, the old man and woman soon went to bed.

Just before dawn, while they were still asleep, a very wonderful thing happened. Suddenly there was the sound of voices in the distance, singing:

"A kind old man walking in the snow,

Gave all his hats to the stone Jizo,

So we bring him gifts with a yo-heave-ho!"

The voices came nearer and nearer, and then the sound of footsteps could be heard in the snow.

The footsteps came right up to the house where the old man and woman were sleeping. And then all at once there was a great noise, as though something heavy had been put down just in front of the house.

The old couple jumped out of bed and ran to the door. When they opened it, what do you suppose they found?

Placed very neatly in front of the house was the biggest and most beautiful rice cake the old couple had ever seen.

"Whoever could have brought us such a wonderful gift?" they asked as they looked around them.

In the snow they saw some tracks leading away from their house. The snow was all tinted with the colors of dawn, and there in the distance, walking through the snow, were the six Jizo statues, still wearing the hats that the old man had given them.

The old man said, "It was the stone Jizo who brought this wonderful rice cake to us!"

The old woman said, "You did them a kind favor when you gave them your hats, so they've brought this rice cake to show their gratitude."

And so the old couple had a very wonderful New Year's Day celebration after all, because they had a wonderful rice cake to share.

THE BOBTAIL MONKEY

Once there was a monkey who was very young and foolish. He was always playing tricks and doing foolish and dangerous things. All the other monkeys kept telling him he ought to be more careful or someday he would get hurt, but he just wouldn't listen to them at all.

One day he was racing through the forest, climbing the highest trees and swinging from the longest vines, and he was so careless that he fell down out of the trees, right into a thorn bush. A long, sharp thorn went right through the tip of his tail.

"Ouch! Oh! Ouch!" he cried, holding his tail. "Oh, how it hurts!" And he began bawling very loudly, for you see the foolish monkey wasn't a brave monkey at all.

Just then a barber came walking by, carrying his razor with him. When the monkey saw him, he said, "Please, Mr. Barber, help me cut this thorn out of my tail."

So the barber got out his razor and started to cut the thorn out. But remember, the foolish monkey wasn't very brave. So when he saw the razor getting near his tail, he yelled, "Oh, it's going to hurt!" And with these words he gave a big jump. The razor went through his tail, cutting the tip of it right off!

When the monkey saw this, he became very angry. "Just look what you've done to my tail!" he said. "You must put my tail back on for me, or else you'll have to give me your razor."

Of course the barber couldn't put the monkey's tail back on, so instead he gave the monkey his razor. Then the foolish monkey went walking away through the forest, carrying the razor with him. He looked very silly with a bobbed tail, but he was so proud of the razor that he didn't even think about his tail.

Presently the monkey came to an old woman who was gathering firewood in the forest. Some of the firewood was too long and she was trying to break it into short pieces to carry home. The monkey watched her for a while. He wanted very much to show someone his beautiful razor, and this seemed like a good chance. So he said, "Look, Granny, I have a wonderful razor, and it's very sharp. You can borrow it if you like to cut your firewood."

The old woman was very pleased. "Thank you very much, Mr. Monkey," she said, and began cutting the wood with the monkey's razor.

Now, a razor is not meant for cutting wood, and very soon the monkey's razor became full of notches and scratches.

When the monkey saw this, he became very angry. "Just look what you've done to my razor!" he said. "You must give it back to me just the way it was before, or else you'll have to give me your firewood."

Of course the old woman couldn't repair the razor, so instead she gave the monkey some of her firewood. Then the foolish monkey went walking away through the forest, carrying the firewood with him. He looked very silly with a bobbed tail, but he was so proud of the firewood that he didn't even think about his tail.

Presently the monkey saw a baker baking senbei. Now, the monkey loved senbei more than anything else and wanted to eat some very badly. So he said, "Look, Aunty, I have some wonderful firewood which is nice and dry. You may borrow it to bake your senbei."

The baker was very pleased, because the wood she was using was green and wouldn't burn well. "Thank you very much, Mr. Monkey," she said. She took the monkey's firewood and put it on the fire.

Now, dry firewood burns very quickly, and the fire burned very brightly. The monkey stood watching until all the senbei were baked. Oh, how good they smelled. He stood there licking his lips. Finally the baker began to take the senbei off the fire. By now all the firewood had been burned to ashes.

When the monkey saw this, he became very angry. "Just look what you've done to my firewood!" he said. "You must give it back to me the way it was before, or else you'll just have to give me some of those senbei that you've baked."

"But how can I give the firewood back?" asked the baker. "You saw it burn up in the fire."

"I can't help that," said the monkey. "You must give it back, or else give me the senbei."

Of course the baker couldn't change the ashes back into firewood, so instead she gave the monkey some of the senbei, piping hot from the oven. Then the foolish monkey went walking away through the forest, nibbling on the delicious senbei. He looked very silly with a bobbed tail, but he was so busy eating that he didn't even think about his tail.

Presently the monkey saw an old man who was carrying a beautiful gong made of brass. Now wouldn't it be wonderful, the monkey told himself, to have a gong like that, so everyone can listen to me. He still had quite a few senbei left, so he said, "Look, Grandpa, I have some delicious senbei here. I'll trade them for that old gong of yours." And he gave the old man one of the senbei to try.

The old man ate the biscuit. It was so delicious that he very much wanted some more. "All right," he said, "you take the gong and I'll take the senbei."

Then the foolish monkey took the gong and climbed to the top of the highest tree in the forest, way up where the branches were thin and bent. He looked very silly with a bobbed tail, but he was so proud of himself and his brass gong that he didn't even think about his tail. He began beating the gong very hard and singing so loudly that all the monkeys in the forest heard him. This is what he sang:

"I'm a handsome little monkey,
The smartest in the land;
With my fine brass gong,
I'm the leader of the band.
Bong! Bong! B-O-N-G!

I had a pretty tail,
Which I traded for a razor,
Which I traded for some wood,
Which I traded for some senbei,
Which I traded for a gong—
A fine brass gong.
Bong! Bong! B-O-N-G!"

How the foolish monkey sang, looking very silly as he waved his bobbed tail in the air where all the other monkeys could see it. But on the last "Bong!" he hit the gong so hard that he fell out of the tree, all the way to the ground, right into another thorn bush!

How all the other monkeys laughed as they pulled the thorns out of him! After that they always called him Bobtail Bong-bong, and never again did he forget about his tail.

The Tuttle Story: "Books to Span the East and West"

Many people are surprised to learn that the world's leading publisher of books on Asia had humble beginnings in the tiny American state of Vermont. The company's founder, Charles E. Tuttle, belonged to a New England family steeped in publishing.

Tuttle's father was a noted antiquarian book dealer in Rutland, Vermont. Young Charles honed his knowledge of the trade working in the family bookstore, and later in the rare books section of Columbia University Library. His passion for beautiful books—old and new—never wavered throughout his long career as a bookseller and publisher.

After graduating from Harvard, Tuttle enlisted in the military and in 1945 was sent to Tokyo to work on General Douglas MacArthur's staff. He was tasked with helping to revive the Japanese publishing industry, which had been utterly devastated by the war. When his tour of duty was completed, he left the military, married a talented and beautiful singer, Reiko Chiba, and in 1948 began several successful business ventures.

To his astonishment, Tuttle discovered that postwar Tokyo was actually a book-lover's paradise. He befriended dealers in the Kanda district and began supplying rare Japanese editions to American libraries. He also imported American books to sell to the thousands of GIs stationed in Japan. By 1949, Tuttle's business was thriving, and he opened Tokyo's very first English-language bookstore in the Takashimaya Department Store in Nihonbashi, to great success. Two years later, he began publishing books to fulfill the growing interest of foreigners in all things Asian.

Though a westerner, Tuttle was hugely instrumental in bringing a knowledge of Japan and Asia to a world hungry for information about the East. By the time of his death in 1993, he had published over 6,000 books on Asian culture, history and art—a legacy honored by Emperor Hirohito in 1983 with the "Order of the Sacred Treasure," the highest honor Japan can bestow upon a non-Japanese.

The Tuttle company today maintains an active backlist of some 1,500 titles, many of which have been continuously in print since the 1950s and 1960s—a great testament to Charles Tuttle's skill as a publisher. More than 60 years after its founding, Tuttle Publishing is more active today than at any time in its history, still inspired by Charles Tuttle's core mission—to publish fine books to span the East and West and provide a greater understanding of each.